JUNGLE
SPROUT

THIS BOOK BELONGS TO

....

FIRST EDITION **ISBN:** 9781092294362

For free coloring pages (featuring the dinosaurs in this book) please email junglesprout@gmail.com quoting promo code 'EasterEggs19'

Everyday this week as soon as Logan awoke he rushed to his mothers nest. He was expecting some new brothers and sisters anytime now.

But today he got a different kind of surprise, a very unusual surprise indeed.

"Hmmmmmm" Logan couldn't understand who would place such a peculiar egg in the nest or why?

He crept towards the nest. Careful not to make a sound. He nudged the egg gently. It was surprisingly light and smelt odd. Very odd indeed.

Maybe Topsy had heard or seen someone.

Before Logan even had a chance to say anything, Topsy screeched with excitement, "Look, look at this strange egg, what could it be?"

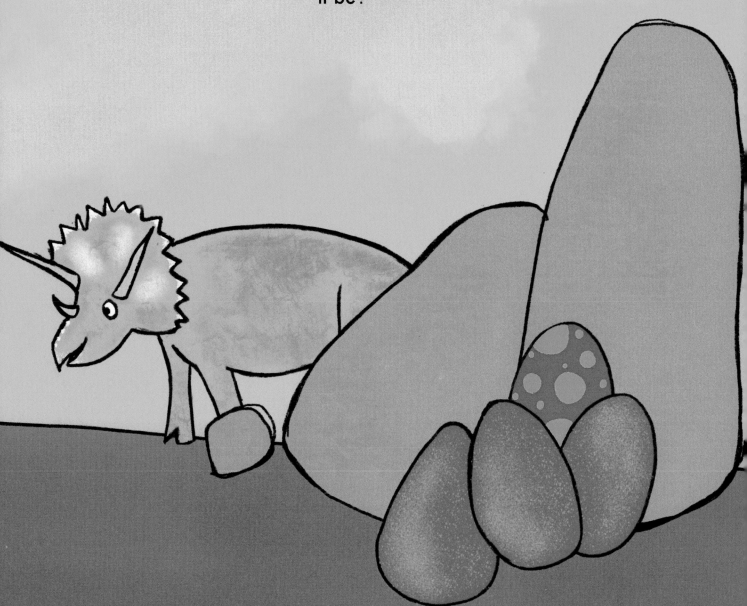

"I did see something running off earlier, it had a fluffy tail, it was round and pink, like nothing I have ever seen before!"

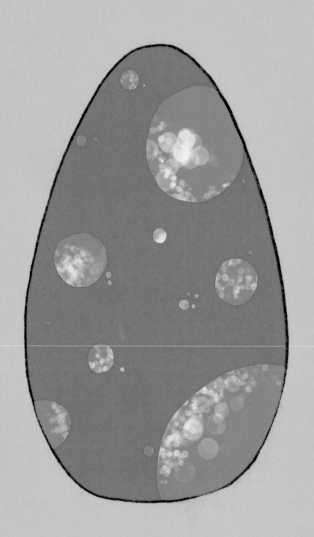

"Lets go and see if Violet has seen anything suspicious"

As they were approaching they could hear her shouting.

"Hey you with the weird ears, come back, you've dropped one of your eggs, h e l l o, little dinosaur, where have you gone?"

What kind of dinosaur has long fluffy pointed ears?

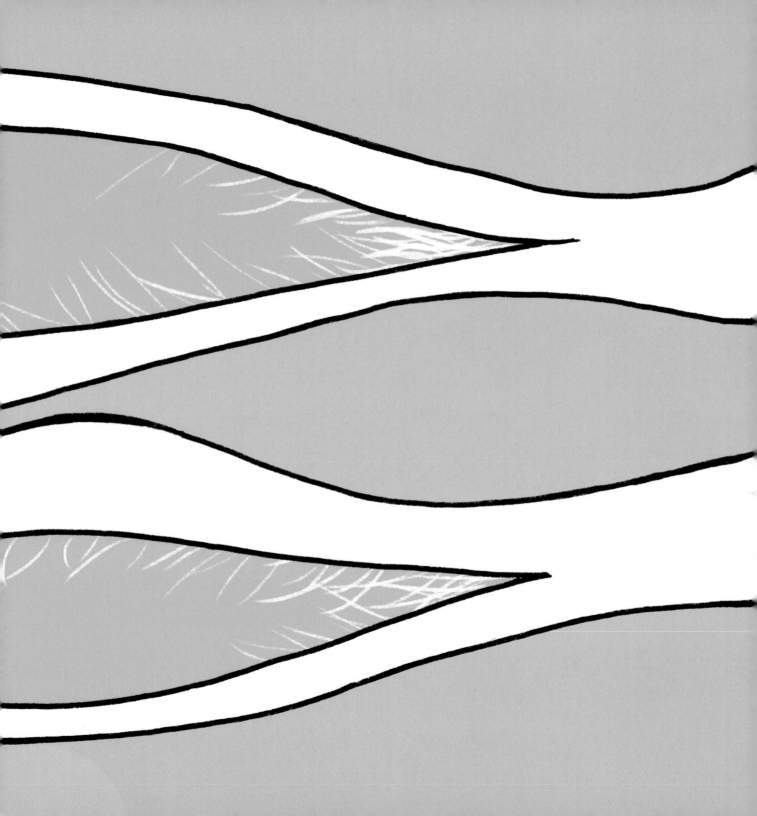

"It's heading towards butterfly creek, the twins might catch it, quick lets go!"

"Cole, Angie, Have you found any unusual eggs ?"
shouted Logan excitedly.
All of us have and we don't know who they belong to,
all we know is they come from a very strange
dinosaur"

"As we were trying to fall asleep, we heard a noise and saw some scary looking teeth, they were square and not sharp at all, when we woke up there were two eggs."

Logan tried to piece together the clues, the tail, the ears, the teeth and the eggs.

They just couldn't work out what creature it could be.

"I think we should go and see old Mendal, he is wise and full of knowledge," insisted Topsy.

They all agreed. They set off on the path towards Mount Ivius where Mendal lived. They had to be careful as they would pass the red mountain. They all clung on to their special but weird eggs.

Cole, Angie and Violet struggled to keep up with Logan and Topsy.
It had been a long morning, with a lot of walking.

Mendal spotted the eggs straight away.
"Wow look at those amazing eggs, Come
inside and have a drink, you all look
exhausted," he said.

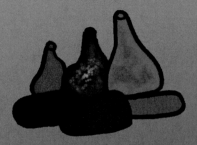

"My Grandad said you are the wisest dinosaur in the land, thats why we have travelled so far to ask you," said Cole.

Mendal chuckled at the little curious dinosaurs, "Well you would have gotten the eggs last year also, but you were too young to remember."

"Why would we have gotten them last year?" Asked Violet. Mendal started to answer "Well...

Legend has it that ever year at spring time, the Easter bunny comes out of hiding and goes all over the land hiding Easter eggs..."

"I have heard about bunnies but I didn't know they laid eggs," said Logan.

"They don't lay eggs, the eggs are supposed to represent new life. Eggs are a sign of birth. Easter is a time to celebrate the beginning of new life," laughed Mendal.

"Just as the seasons change all year round, Easter is about the seasons of our lives changing, it reminds us that there is hope for our future, especially after a difficult struggle."

"Wow, what an amazing time of year easter is, thank you so much Mendal, we just knew we could rely on you," said Topsy.

"But what are we supposed to do with Easter eggs?" asked Angie.

"Well EAT them off course," replied Mendal.

"Eat them!" The little dinosaurs said in horror.

"Yes, they are made of chocolate!"

Mmmmmm yummy! All the dinosaurs enjoyed their delicious Easter eggs.

"Time for you little ones to get back to your families so you can all celebrate together," Mendal said.

What an amazing adventure they had on this beautiful spring morning.

As they were leaving Topsy asked Mendal, "Why don't you come back with us to celebrate, you must be lonely here by yourself"

"Oh no, Don't worry about me little ones, I already have plans, I will be celebrating with my neighbour later"...

"Okay, Thanks again, Happy Easter! Goodbye Mendal."

Made in the USA
Columbia, SC
11 April 2019